Tisha B'Av
A Jerusalem Journey

To all the people of Jerusalem, may you know peace soon.
Thanks to my parents Cecily and Martin Slater, husband Shmuel and
daughter Aravah for all their love and support.
– A.O.

Dedicated to all the people in the world working toward a future of peace
– E.A.

Map on page 32 courtesy of Western Walls Heritage Foundation.

Text copyright © 2017 Allison Ofanansky
Photos copyright © 2017 by Eliyahu Alpern www.tziloom.com

Kar-Ben Publishing
A division of Lerner Publishing Group, Inc.
241 First Avenue North
Minneapolis, MN 55401 U.S.A.
1-800-4-KARBEN

Website address: www.karben.com

Library of Congress Cataloging-in-Publication Data

Names: Ofanansky, Allison, author. | Alpern, Eliyahu, photographer.
Title: Tisha b'Av : a Jerusalem journey / by Allison Ofanansky ; photographs by Eliyahu Alpern.
Description: Minneapolis : Kar-Ben Publishing, [2017] | Summary: "A family explores the city of Jerusalem on the eve of Tisha B'Av, which commemorates the destruction of the Temples in Jerusalem. Their guides take them outside the city, underground to see buried portions of the Western Wall, and to a sifting project and teach them the history of the holiday"—Provided by publisher.
Identifiers: LCCN 2016009547 (print) | LCCN 2016034222 (ebook) | ISBN 9781467789301 (lb : alk. paper) | ISBN 9781512427196 (eb pdf)
Subjects: | CYAC: Ninth of Av—Fiction. | Judaism—Customs and practices—Fiction. | Jerusalem—Fiction. | Israel—Fiction.
Classification: LCC PZ7.O31 Tis 2017 (print) | LCC PZ7.O31 (ebook) | DDC [E]—dc23

LC record available at https://lccn.loc.gov/2016009547

Manufactured in the United States of America
1-38116-19960-7/25/2016

Tisha B'Av
A Jerusalem Journey

By Allison Ofanasky
Photographs by Eiyahu Alpern

KAR-BEN
PUBLISHING

I stand with my little brother Nitzan and cousin Aravah on the Mount of Olives and look through my binoculars at the city of Jerusalem. "Can you imagine what this used to look like long ago?" Aravah says. "There were no cars or roads. All of Jerusalem was inside those walls. The rest was open fields and trees. And the Temple stood over there in the Old City."

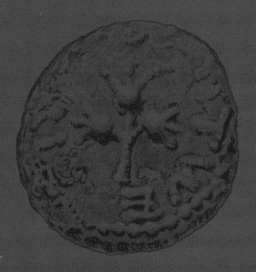

"Did you ever go to the Temple?" Nitzan asks her.

Aravah laughs. "No! It was destroyed thousands of years ago. But we remember it every year, on Tisha B'Av, which starts tonight."

"How can we remember something we never experienced?" I wonder.

"Let's go, kids!" my aunt calls. "It's time to move on to our next stop in our Tisha B'Av tour."

Before we go, Aravah snaps a selfie of us with Jerusalem in the background.

We go into the Old City, to the Western Wall of the Temple, which we call the Kotel. I press my face against the stones and say a little prayer.

"For a long time, the Western Wall of the Temple was the only part of the wall that could be seen," says my aunt. "But archaeologists are uncovering more of it every day."

We walk to Robinson's Arch. "Stones were knocked down when the Roman army destroyed the Temple, more than 2000 years ago," says my aunt. "And now we're going to see parts of the Wall that are buried!"

The day is hot but we go into a cool tunnel. "You picked a great day to visit," says our guide Yehuda. "Even though Tisha B'Av is a sad day in Jewish history, we will have fun exploring Jerusalem underground." He leads us into a room with a model of a mountain. "This is the mountain on which Jerusalem is built. It is said that some of the stories in the Bible took place here."

"King David made Jerusalem the capital of his kingdom and his son, King Solomon, built the First Temple on this hilltop. The First Temple was destroyed by the Babylonians on Tisha B'Av.

"Seventy years later, the Jewish People came back to Jerusalem. They flattened the whole mountaintop into a platform as big as 30 football fields, with walls all around it. A big, beautiful Temple was built on the platform. Then, along came the Roman Army and destroyed it…"

"On Tisha B'Av!" I shout.

"Right," says Yehuda.

"What's on the Temple Mount now?" Nitzan asks. "There are mosques, including one with a gold dome. This mountain is holy in Islam, too."

"To make it easier to get up to the mosque, the Muslims built a city on arches, and much of the wall was covered up."

"Now I'm going to take you further underneath the city, to see the buried sections of the wall — and more!" Yehuda leads us down a long passage.

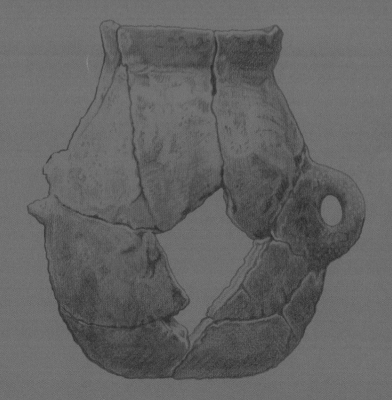

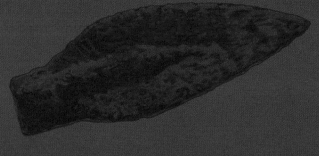

We see arches and pillars and places people used to bathe.

"Look at this giant stone," Yehuda says. He tells me to stand at one end of the stone and Nitzan at the other. "This stone weighs as much as 600 elephants."

I ask, "How did they move stones this big before they had machines?"

"They used oxen to haul them with ropes, and rolled them on logs. Let's do an experiment." Yehuda tells my aunt, cousin, and brother to lie on the ground, and me to lie on top of them. "Now roll!" I feel myself move down the line.

We continue our tour. I stop with a yelp as the floor seems to drop away. Yehuda says, "This window lets you look further down. You can see stones that fell into what used to be a marketplace."

The path narrows. "This was once an aqueduct," says Yehuda, "a channel that fed water into a pool."

We come into a wide room with a big pool. "This was part of a moat around a fortress King Herod built." We laugh when Nitzan says he wants to go swimming.

We thank Yehuda for the tour. "Come back in a few years," he says. "We are finding new things all the time!"

For the next part of our Tisha B'Av tour, we drive across the city, and park near a big tent. I read the sign, **Welcome to the Temple Mount Sifting Project**.

"Now we are going to be archaeologists ourselves!" says my aunt.

Our guide Aaron explains, "You are going to help us sift through dirt that was dug out of the Temple Mount. We are looking for things that were buried long ago."

Aaron shows us some of the things they have found: coins, pottery, game pieces, bones, jewelry, and mosaic tiles. Archaeologists study these items to figure out what they are, how old they are, and who made them.

"I'm going to find King Solomon's crown!" I say.

Aaron laughs. "That would be wonderful."

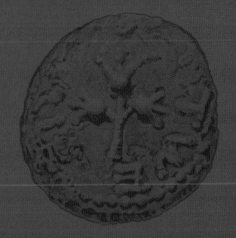

We learn how to
sift like archaeologists.
First, I bring over a
bucket of dirt.

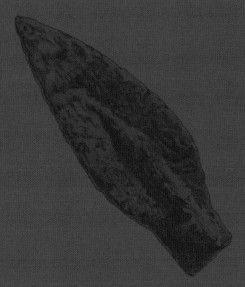

At our sifting station, we dump the bucket onto a screen and spray off the dirt with a hose.

Aaron tells what to look for. He shows us how to sort our finds into a muffin tin with compartments for pottery, glass, metal, mosaics, bones, and unusual stones.

I run my fingers through the rubble on the screen. Something catches my eye.

I look at it with a magnifying glass. I think it's a piece of pottery!

We find glass and bits
of bone and rocks which
have been carved or
painted. Aaron checks
to make sure we didn't
miss anything and that it's
sorted correctly.

We put our finds
into plastic buckets,

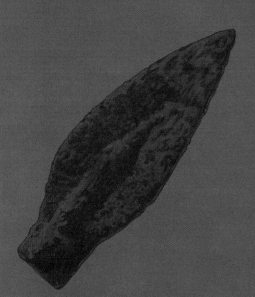

חרסים
Pottery

זכוכית
Glass

עצמות
Bones

and dump the
leftovers into a
wheelbarrow.

שולחן ארכיאולוג
Archaeologist's Tabl

When we finish, I get to sit at the Archaeologist's Table!

"It's time to go," my aunt says. "I need to eat dinner before Tisha B'Av starts."

"Why?" I ask.

"We fast on Tisha B'Av — which means we don't eat or drink — to remind ourselves that this is a sad day for the Jewish people."

"Do I have to fast?"

"No. Kids don't fast. You can remember the Temples by thinking about everything we've learned today."

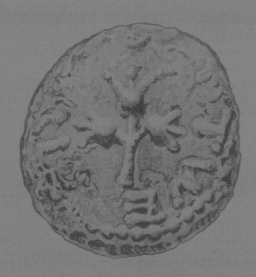

After dark, we go back to the Western Wall. Tisha B'Av has begun. People are starting to gather to pray. Some are sitting on the ground instead of in chairs. That's another Tisha B'Av custom. We sit on the ground, too.

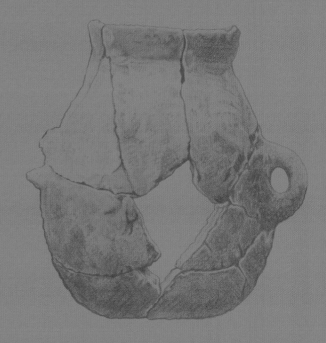

When we get home, I take out my blocks and build a big Temple with arches and tunnels like the ones we visited.

Just as I finish, my baby brother crawls over.

Uh-oh. My Temple crashes to the ground. But that's what Tisha B'Av is all about. How did my baby brother know?

ABOUT TISHA B'AV

Tisha B'Av, the 9th day of the Hebrew month of Av *(tisha means 9 in Hebrew)*, is a day for mourning the loss of the ancient Temples in Jerusalem. According to Jewish tradition, both of the Temples were destroyed on that day: the first in 586 BCE and the second in 70 AD. For many centuries, the Temples were the center of Jewish life, and where people came to pray on the holidays of Sukkot, Passover and Shavuot.

There are many Tisha B'Av traditions: fasting, not wearing leather, not swimming, and sitting on low stools or on the floor. In the synagogue, we read a section of the Bible called Eicha (Lamentations) which deals with the destruction of the Temples.

Although historians question whether the two Temples were actually destroyed on this date, Tisha B'Av has become a symbol of Jewish suffering and loss. Over the centuries, other tragic events have come to be commemorated on this day, including the Crusades, the expulsion of the Jews from Spain, and the Holocaust. In modern times, Tisha B'Av has become a day to reflect on the suffering that still occurs in our world.

 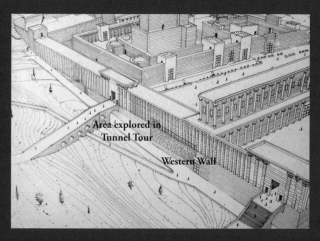

Western Wall of the Temple Mount in Jerusalem during the Second Temple Era after King Herod's expansion.

ABOUT THE AUTHOR AND PHOTOGRAPHER

Allison Ofanansky lives in Israel with her husband Shmuel and their daughter Aravah. Photographer **Eliyahu Alpern** has been interested in food, travel and photography since childhood. His photographic specialty is 360-degree panoramic images of Israel. He lives in the Upper Galilee with his family. This is the sixth book in their series about Jewish holidays and nature in Israel.